A NEW HOPE

BY ACE LANDERS   ILLUSTRATED BY DAVID WHITE

SCHOLASTIC INC.

PUBLISHED BY SCHOLASTIC INC., PUBLISHERS SINCE 1920. SCHOLASTIC AND ASSOCIATED LOGOS ARE TRADEMARKS
AND/OR REGISTERED TRADEMARKS OF SCHOLASTIC INC.

ISBN 978-0545-80135-5

10 9 8 7 6 5 4 3 2 1   16 17 18 19 20

PRINTED IN THE U.S.A.   40
FIRST PRINTING 2016

BOOK DESIGN BY ERIN MCMAHON

**A LONG TIME AGO
IN A GALAXY FAR, FAR AWAY. . . .**

*The evil Darth Vader was
hunting a brave young princess
who had stolen the instructions
for the Empire's wickedest
weapon* *the Death Star.*

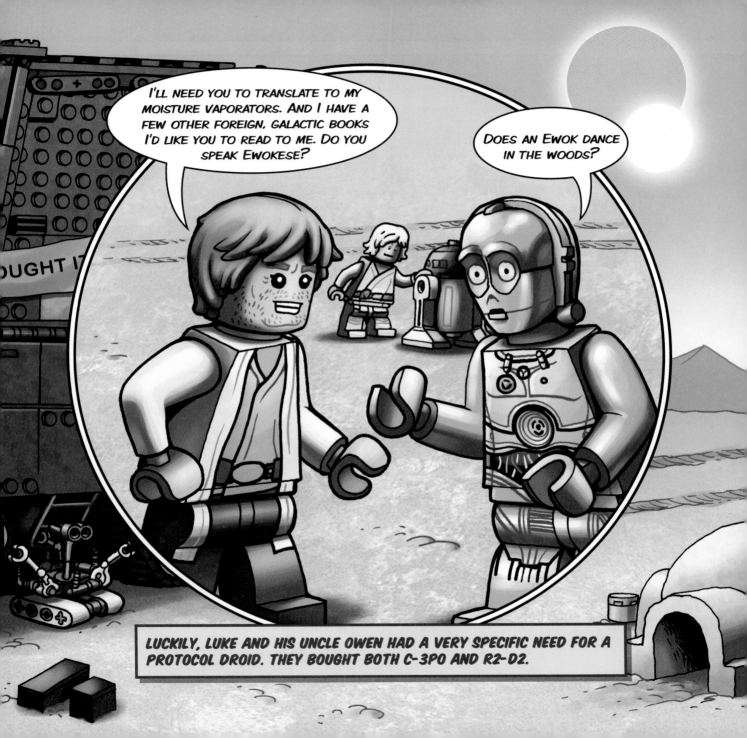

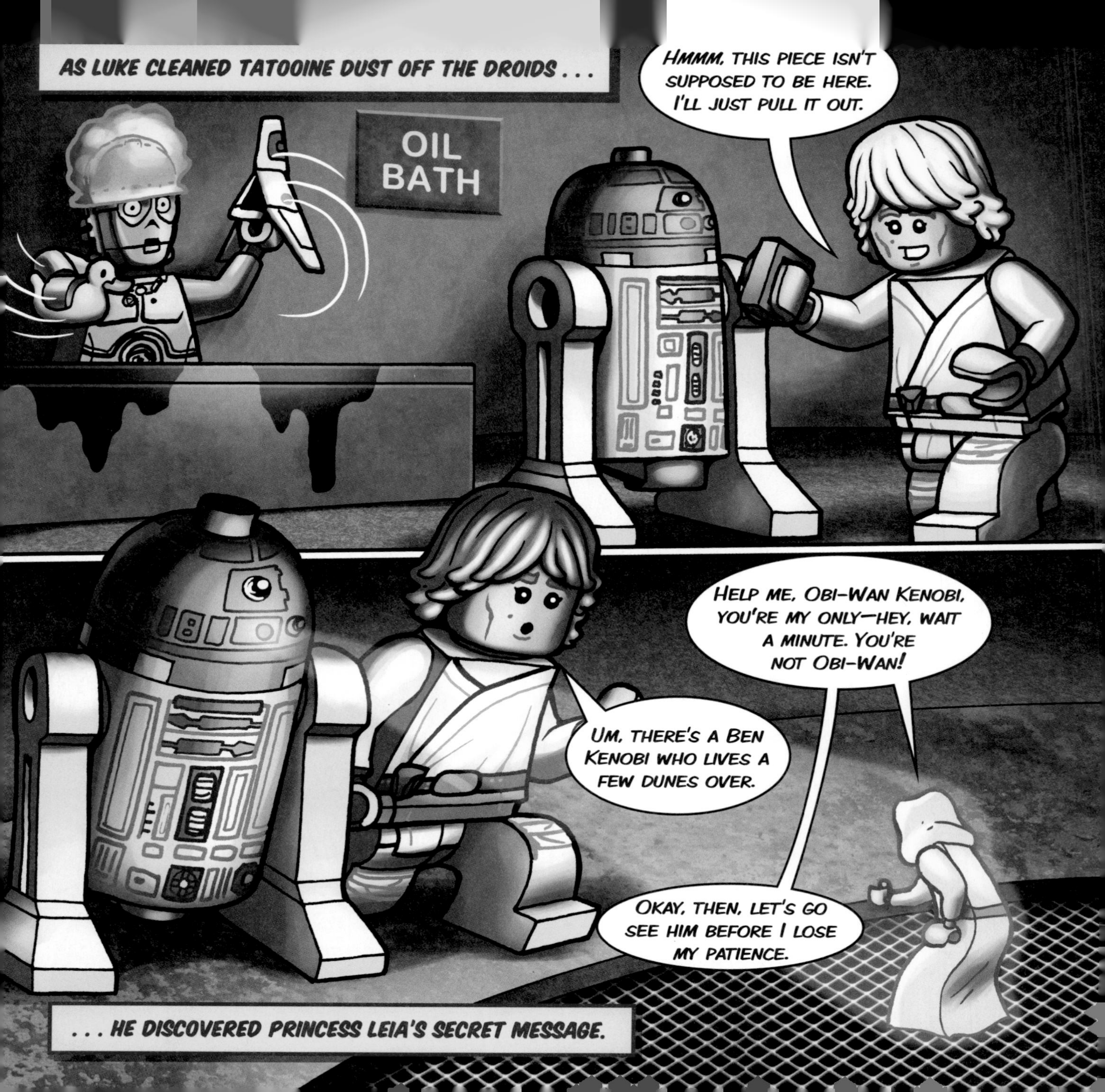
AS LUKE CLEANED TATOOINE DUST OFF THE DROIDS . . .
OIL BATH
HMMM, THIS PIECE ISN'T SUPPOSED TO BE HERE. I'LL JUST PULL IT OUT.
HELP ME, OBI-WAN KENOBI, YOU'RE MY ONLY—HEY, WAIT A MINUTE. YOU'RE NOT OBI-WAN!
UM, THERE'S A BEN KENOBI WHO LIVES A FEW DUNES OVER.
OKAY, THEN, LET'S GO SEE HIM BEFORE I LOSE MY PATIENCE.
. . . HE DISCOVERED PRINCESS LEIA'S SECRET MESSAGE.

LUKE AND THE DROIDS RUSHED OVER TO KENOBI'S HOUSE. THERE, LUKE LEARNED THAT NOT ONLY WAS BEN KENOBI ONCE A JEDI KNIGHT, BUT THAT LUKE'S FATHER WAS A JEDI, TOO! AND NOW IT WAS UP TO LUKE AND OBI-WAN (BEN) KENOBI TO DESTROY THE DEATH STAR AND STOP THE EMPIRE BEFORE THEY TOOK CONTROL OF THE GALAXY.

LUKE, THIS IS A LOT TO TAKE IN, ARE YOU OKAY?

ARE YOU KIDDING? THIS IS THE BEST. DAY. EVER!

GET A MOVE ON, GUYS! I'M TIRED OF WAITING, AND THE DEATH STAR ISN'T GOING TO DESTROY ITSELF!

THERE WAS ONLY ONE PLACE ON TATOOINE TO FIND SOMEONE THAT CRAZY: MOS EISLEY. THIS CITY WAS THE ROOTIN'EST, TOOTIN'EST OUTLAW TOWN IN THE GALAXY.
YOU DROIDS AREN'T ALLOWED IN HERE.
BLEEP! BOOP!
WE AIN'T THE DROIDS YOU'RE LOOKING FOR, PARDNER.
THIS NEXT SONG GOES OUT TO THE OUTLAWS IN THE BACK WHO WANT TO DO THE ROBOT DANCE!

IN NO TIME, HAN SOLO AND CHEWBACCA AGREED TO HELP SAVE THE PRINCESS. WITH THE TEAM INTACT, THE CREW BOARDED THE *MILLENNIUM FALCON* AND BLASTED OFF.

WOW, THIS IS A KEEPER.

CAREFUL, KID. DON'T PICK APART MY BUCKET OF BOLTS—I MEAN, SPACESHIP.

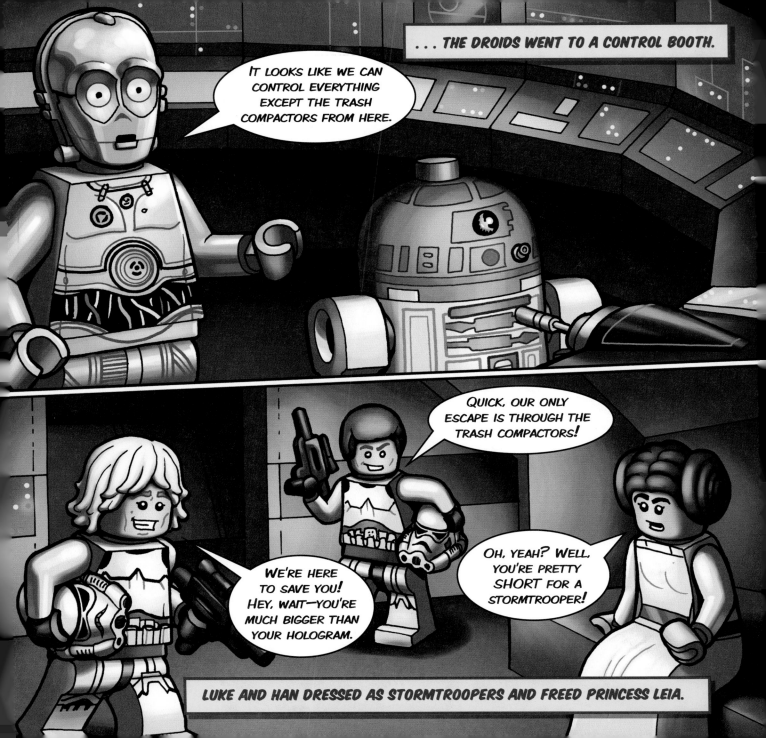

MEANWHILE, DARTH VADER FOUND HIS OLD NEMESIS, OBI-WAN KENOBI. THE SITH LORD AND THE JEDI BATTLED UNTIL KENOBI WAS SURE THAT LUKE, LEIA, AND THE CREW HAD SAFELY ESCAPED.

THE X-WINGS STRUCK FIRST, BUT THEY WERE OVERPOWERED BY HUNDREDS OF TIE FIGHTERS. LUKE MANAGED TO DODGE AND WEAVE HIS WAY TOWARD THE DEATH STAR'S ONE WEAK SPOT.

BUT DARTH VADER DID NOT GIVE UP SO EASILY! HE CHASED LUKE AND WAS JUST ABOUT TO BLAST HIM OUT OF THE GALAXY . . .
THERE'S NO ESCAPE NOW.
ARTOO, DUMP THOSE PIECES I'VE BEEN COLLECTING. THEY'RE SLOWING US DOWN.
. . . WHEN LUKE GAVE HIM A SPECIAL SURPRISE!